Nerdi Bunny

And the Busy Bee
Bully Bear Business

by

Aisha Toombs

Printed in the United States of America

Second Printing, 2019

ISBN: 978-1-7337947-0-1

For daring to love me, and encouraging me to dream...
For my Hunny-Lamb and my Meem.

Contents

Not Your Average Bunny

NERDI BUNNY LOVES TO READ! Today's titles included a non-fiction selection called *Whether the Weather* and two fictional stories, *The Romance of Mew and Squeak* and *Hoot's the Boss!* She had been spending her school vacation sitting in her favorite chair surrounded by daily newspapers and books. Nerdi treasured these last few days of quiet because soon the twins, Artsy and Sporty, would return home from camp, filling the house with stories of their adventures and creating new mischief.

Nerdi started her afternoon reading with headlines from today's paper:

HONEY AND HARVEST FESTIVAL IN JEOPARDY!

BEE TALKS BREAK DOWN!

SHORTAGE SHUTS DOWN BURROW SWEET SHOPS!

"Oh no," Nerdi sighed to herself, "no festival this year AND no sweets? Our house without treats will be trouble for sure. I wonder if there's anything I can do to help."

Nerdi was an excellent helper. On vacation last year a pair of pandas had car trouble and Nerdi was able to fix it in a jiffy because of her subscription to *Modern Bunny Mechanics*. When the penguins who ran the ice cream shop in town caught the flu, Nerdi cooked a carrot and krill soup she had read about on BunnyMD.com that had them flopping around in no time.

At the end of the school year her class needed help saving money for the school trip. Nerdi showed everyone how to turn thirty-three cents from their lunch money into almost three dollars in three days. It worked so well that the class had enough money left over to install a bunny bounce in the schoolyard! If you were afraid of pickles—well, Nerdi hasn't met anyone like that just yet, but if she did, she could help them through that predicament, too!

This afternoon as Nerdi settled into her reading, Mama Bunny prepared their favorite lunch—a delicious tomato and basil salad. Tomatoes were Nerdi's favorite food. Now, I know what you're thinking. Nerdi is a bunny. Bunnies like carrots. Nerdi, though, is not your typical bunny. Nerdi probably loves tomatoes as much as she loves books! Tomato salad, tomato soup, tomato slices. She was even working on a recipe for tomato ice cream for this year's Honey and Harvest Festival, which, according to the article she read, might be canceled.

"Nerdine?" Mama called from the kitchen. Mama was the only one who called Nerdi by her real name.

"Yes?" she replied with her nose still in today's paper.

"Would you please go into the vegetable garden and pick some tomatoes?" Mama asked. "And yes, I know you're reading, but you have to feed your brain AND your body, Nerdine."

As smart as Nerdi was, she knew Mama knew best. Nerdi folded the pages back to hold her place and set the paper on the seat. She was just getting to the part about the bees, which reminded her to put on her netted bonnet and gloves before picking up the vegetable basket.

"How many tomatoes would you like, Mama?"

"Two would do nicely," she answered, and Nerdi picked up the basket and went out to the garden. When Nerdi reached the tomato patch something was very wrong. Her pulse raced as she went from plant to plant. Nothing. As she frantically checked each plant along the trellis her breathing quickened. Still nothing. Suddenly, the garden began to spin. Things got very dark and she shouted, "All the tomatoes are gone!"

What's the Buzz?

ONLY A FEW MINUTES HAD passed when Nerdi woke up. She thought she had imagined things. No way did the garden NOT have any tomatoes. She was being silly. Or maybe the sun was too hot and she needed hydration. Nerdi sat up slowly and looked around, but it wasn't a dream. Every tomato plant in the patch had green leaves, nothing red, and Nerdi felt lost in the sea of green.

"Looking for something?" buzzed a voice from one of the leaves. "That's too bad, because there will be no more tomatoes until we get what we need!"

Nerdi hopped to her feet and trembled. Her light-headedness from the absence of tomatoes disappeared. She knew that sound too well and was glad she had put on her netted bonnet and gloves. On the leaves she saw two very angry bees and, not wanting to upset them further, she slowly began to hop away.

"Where are you going?" asked one of the bees as it zinged up to Nerdi's glasses and sat on the bar across her nose. Nerdi twitched her whiskers, shook her head, raised her paw, closed her eyes, and prepared to strike.

"Please don't swat me," the bee yelled as it threw up a few of its legs, bracing for the blow. "Swatting is why this whole mess got started. The name's Jimmy and I promise not to sting ya. Look!"

Jimmy hovered above Nerdi's nose. She slowly opened one of her eyes, but kept her paw raised to swat if she had to. When Jimmy could see that she was looking, he buzzed around and shook his bumblebee butt. "See, I don't even have a stinger," he said as he wiggled repeatedly. Nerdi relaxed, her ears going floppy as she breathed out and slowly put down her paw.

"No stinger? Why don't you have a stinger?" she asked.

"I'm a guy," Jimmy replied. "We don't have stingers. But Cleo over there—she does."

Nerdi's ears stood up like two arrows pointing in the direction she should run. She could be friends with Jimmy because he didn't have a stinger. Cleo was a different story.

"Is she coming up here too?" Nerdi asked as her paw returned to the striking position.

"Not if she's going to get swatted."

"Well…" Nerdi hesitated. Part of her wanted to be brave. Part of her was really hungry and wanted to know what happened to the tomatoes. Part of her wanted to swat both of the bees and bound screaming back into the house, never to go in the vegetable garden again, but that would mean no tomato salad and she wasn't comfortable with that. After a brief moment of reflection, she concluded that tomatoes were worth the risk.

"Well, I promise not to swat if Cleo promises not to sting."

"Hey, Cleo!" Jimmy yelled. "It's safe to come on up—the bunny won't swat ya if ya put a cap on that stinger!"

Cleo, very fuzzy and very yellow, flew up to where Jimmy was sitting.

"So pretty," Nerdi thought out loud to no one in particular, but she was soon zapped back to reality at the sight of Cleo's shiny black stinger. Cleo noticed Nerdi's fur stand straight up and quickly put a safety cap on it and then sat next to Jimmy.

"We just want to talk," Cleo said with a kindness in her tone that reminded Nerdi of Mama.

"About what happened to the tomatoes?" Nerdi asked.

"Not just your tomatoes," Cleo continued, "but everyone's tomatoes, and honey, and clover, and almonds, and…"

"The point is," Jimmy interrupted, "the food supply in Cottontail Burrow is in trouble. If the bees don't get back to business, it's going to get very hard around here for everyone."

Nerdi thought back to the story she was reading before Mama sent her to the garden. Things began to make sense. If the bees had stopped working, then that explains why the sweet shops were closing. If the bees had stopped working, that would also explain why there were no tomatoes in the vegetable garden. Nerdi couldn't decide which was worse: a day without tomatoes or weeks with the twins without sweets and treats.

Brain Itch, Bunny Twitch

NERDI EXCUSED HERSELF AND SCURRIED back into the house. Mama was sitting at the table with a big bowl of basil.

"You must not be very hungry. What took so long, Nerdine?" Mama asked.

"We have a situation. I think you should come outside, Mama." Nerdi helped Mama bring a chair out into the garden. Nerdi then took off her bonnet and gloves and put them in the basket.

"Where are all the tomatoes, Nerdine?" Mama asked.

"The bees have stopped working," Nerdi replied.

Mama took a seat and slumped down in her chair. "If the bees aren't working, that could be disastrous, Nerdine. How do you know they've stopped working?"

"From two bees I met in the garden, Cleo and Jimmy. I think they'll explain a bit more, but you must promise not to swat at them."

"I'm not a swatter, Nerdine. And you know better than to swat, too." Nerdi felt her whiskers drop and her cheeks flush. "Your new friends are safe with me."

Cleo and Jimmy whizzed up to where Mama sat in her chair and settled on the back of her paw. Many of the bees that were staying out of sight saw this and were amazed. Usually the other beasts in the burrow reacted with swats and screams if a bee got that close to them, but Nerdi and her mama were as cool as cucumbers.

"You aren't afraid of us?" Cleo asked with a very surprised tone.

"No, bees are welcome in our garden. Without you, how else are we able to have fresh fruits and vegetables all year long? You are very important. Nerdine knows that too, but she was stung as a little bunny and is still a bit afraid when she sees bees."

Cleo smiled at Mama and Nerdine. "Your mama is very kind to make us feel welcome and safe," said Cleo. "Maybe if the queens knew there were folks like you and your mama, we could get back to work in time for the Honey and Harvest Festival."

The Honey and Harvest Festival was the biggest event in Cottontail Burrow. The weather there was always warm, so the bees were able to work and make honey all year round. Farmers in the burrow knew how to plant crops in a special way so that things like tomatoes, apples, avocados, and berries were always in season. At the Honey and Harvest Festival everyone would bring their best recipes, and prizes and ribbons were awarded for the best-tasting dishes. At the end of the day, after all the prizes were given out, everyone would then gather in the park to share all the delicious food.

"The queen bees control the hives. They tell us when to work and when to rest. We have been resting for weeks now because when we try to do our job, folks swat at us and tell us to go away," said Jimmy. "Many of us have gotten our wings broken or worse. Folks around here seem to think all bees are bad or worse—wasps!"

"Bumbles and honeybees are here to help things grow, not hurt anyone," said Cleo. "At least not on purpose."

Suddenly the garden was all abuzz. Hundreds of bumblebees and honeybees rose up. Some carried signs that said things like "Don't hurt the bees" and "Save the bumbles." Nerdi's whiskers started twitching, but she never lifted her paw. She was listening closely to Jimmy and Cleo.

"We can't do our job with all the harmful sprays and swatting at us—so we're not working at all!" said Cleo.

Then the chanting began:

"Hurting bees isn't funny! No tomatoes AND no honey!"

"When you swat that paw or finger, that makes us use our stinger!"

Over and over and over they sang.

As the chanting grew louder, Nerdi pondered very hard. Something had to be done. What good was a basil and tomato salad without tomatoes? Also, the Honey and Harvest Festival had never been canceled before. Everyone looked forward to it every year. Her twin siblings, Artsy and Sporty, would return from camp soon expecting Mama's honey cake, and there would be no honey cakes? The horror!

Nerdi's whiskers grew more and more twitchy. Mama knew that meant Nerdi was thinking very, very hard about something.

"When that brain starts to itch, the bunny gets a twitch," said Mama. "I think Nerdine may have a plan."

"What's up, bunny? What ya thinking about?" asked Jimmy.

"I think I can get the bees back to work, but I need help. Do you think your queens would meet with me tomorrow?"

"I don't know," Cleo replied. "The queens rarely come out of the hive. It's for their own safety."

"They might make an exception for this, though," said Jimmy. "Besides, the bunny is cool. She won't hurt them."

"All right," said Cleo. "We'll ask them to get together and meet you here in the garden in the morning."

Jimmy suddenly became very excited and flew above the chanting bees. "EVERYBODY ZIP IT!!" Jimmy buzzed as loud as he could. The garden hushed. Not a buzz or chant could be heard. "The stoppage may soon be over! The bunny has an idea!"

Problem Solved!

NERDI AWOKE THE NEXT MORNING to bright sunshine filling her room. She thought this was a good sign of how well the day was going to go. If the sunshine wasn't enough of a hint, when she went to the mirror to fluff her ears, she got them perfectly fluffed with just the right amount of perk on the first try. After Jimmy's announcement yesterday, the pressure was on and she didn't want to disappoint the bees. It wasn't just because that would mean hundreds of angry stingers pointing in her direction, but she also didn't want to let her new friends Jimmy and Cleo down. Nerdi made her way to the kitchen where Mama was preparing breakfast. The aroma of warm buttery toast and hot peppermint tea filled the room. Mama made the best peppermint tea. Nerdi poured herself a mug. As she took a sip and prepared to savor the sweet, hot goodness, she gagged and had to force it down her throat.

"Mama!" Nerdi choked as she madly wiped her tongue with her napkin. "What's wrong with the tea? Did you forget how to make it?"

Mama brought over some toast to the table and sat down. "No, Nerdine, I didn't forget how to make the tea, but given our current situation I thought it best to save what little honey we have left." Once again, Mama knew best.

Nerdi picked up the morning paper and read the headline:

HONEY FESTIVAL CANCELED!
MAYOR BEAR BAWLS OVER BARREN
HONEY BARRELS!

"Oh no, Mama. They've canceled the festival!"

"Things have gotten quite serious," Mama said. "I know you have an idea on how to fix all this and I hope it works."

Nerdi read the story. Mayor Bear was quite broken up about canceling the Honey Harvest Festival. She could understand why, of course. No one loved honey more than bears.

"Bears! That's it!" Nerdi shouted as she bounced around the kitchen. She developed a case of the hippity-hops. When bunnies become very excited, they get the hippity-hops. It's like the hiccups, but in their feet.

"Nerdine! What's gotten into you?"

"Bears, Mama!"

Boing! Off the chair.

"Bears love honey!"

Boing! On the counter!

"Our mayor is a bear!"

Boing! Back on the chair.

"I don't understand, Nerdine," Mama said.

"That's how I can help the bees! May I make a call?" Nerdi asked.

"When you stop bouncing around the kitchen," Mama replied, "yes, you may."

Nerdi took a sip from her tea. The peppermint calmed her down instantly but she missed the sweetness of the honey. Nerdi dialed the mayor's office.

"Mayor Bear's office," sniffled a voice on the other end. "How may I help you?"

"Hello, Mister Mayor. My name is Nerdine Bunny and I read the story this morning in the paper about the festival being canceled and I think I can help you."

"Really?" sniffed the mayor. "Do you have honey? And how did you know it was me?"

Nerdi didn't want to offend the mayor by telling him that she knew it was him because he was still crying, so she skipped responding to that question.

"Honey? Not exactly, sir, but I know how you could get more."

"I'm listening."

"Well, to start, I think you and the bees should meet to discuss what they need."

"What they need?" the mayor angrily replied. "I had to drink my tea this morning with no honey! Do you know what that tastes like?" Nerdi understood very well what the mayor's tea tasted like, but she didn't interrupt him. "It was terrible! I can't focus on what the bees need! They *need* to get back to work and start making honey again. President O'Llama is coming today. He'll be here for his vacation and he is supposed to be our honored guest at this year's festival. We might have to cancel the visit because of this nonsense."

"With all due respect, sir, it's that kind of attitude that has gotten us into this mess in the first place." Nerdi continued, "Bees aren't pests. They are an important part of our community. They need our respect. No, they deserve our respect. What they do goes beyond just honey. Soon we're going to run out of other things, too."

"What?" the mayor said. "Not just honey?"

"No, sir. Honey, apples, carrots, almonds, clover, berries…"

"Enough! You've made your point. Very well, I'll agree to meet with these bees, but not all of them!"

"Of course not all of them, Mr. Mayor. That would be dangerous."

"The queens and perhaps a few representatives. Until we figure out what the bees need, we don't want folks to get scared and think it's a swarm or something."

"May I make a suggestion?" Nerdi asked.

"I should hire you with all your suggestions. Go on."

"Well," Nerdi continued, "when you meet, maybe you should come up with rules. Not just for the bees, but for us to follow as well."

"Hmm. That's a good idea! President O'Llama will be here this afternoon. He's here on vacation until after the festival. Maybe he can help us figure out what the rules should be. He's good at that sort of thing."

"Shouldn't we let him enjoy his vacation?"

"It won't be much of a vacation without sweets and treats! Call me back when you've set it up, Nadine."

"Nerdine," she corrected him. "And thank you very much, Mr. Mayor."

Nerdi hung up the phone just as Mama returned to the kitchen wearing her coat and gloves.

"I'm off to go pick up your sister and brother from camp. While I'm away, Nana is in charge."

"Mama! The mayor wants to meet with the bees AND President O'Llama will be here this afternoon, so he might help too! This may all get sorted out before supper!"

"That's wonderful news, Nerdine!" Mama said as she hugged her and kissed her on the nose. "I knew you would figure something out. You always do. I'll be back in a day or two."

And with a kiss on the cheek, Mama was off and Nerdi dashed to the garden to share the good news with Cleo, Jimmy, and the queen bees.

Napped!

Nerdi sat on a patch of grass and waited for Jimmy, Cleo, and the queens. The sun shone bright and the sky was a soft blue with big puffy clouds. It was very quiet today in the garden. While waiting for Jimmy and Cleo, Nerdi decided to lie down on the grass and figure out what each cloud shape reminded her of. The first cloud was round and fat with wisps coming out of the top. Nerdi thought that one looked like a tomato. The second cloud was rounder and fatter than the first. She thought that one looked like a bigger tomato. Before she could figure out what type of tomato the third cloud reminded her of, she heard very sad buzzing coming toward her. Nerdi sat up and saw Jimmy and a very upset Cleo flying slowly in her direction.

"What's wrong, Cleo?"

"*Buzzzzzz*, boo-hoo-hoo, *buzzzzzz*, queens, *buzzzzzzzzz*, today, boo-hoo-hooo, gone! *Buzzzzzz!*" Cleo tried to explain, but between the buzzing and the crying, it was very hard to understand anything Cleo said.

"Jimmy? What's wrong? I have good news. The mayor wants to meet with you and the queens, but the queens aren't here."

Jimmy's eyes were full of water. He wiped them before he spoke. "The queens were gonna come with us this morning. But last night…"

"What happened last night?"

"Last night they were taken. The queens and some of the other bees were taken! It was hard to leave the hive this morning," Jimmy continued. "The queens give us tasks to do each day. We usually can't leave the hive without their permission."

Nerdi thought it was very quiet in the garden this morning. You could hear the cool breeze move through the trees like whispers. There was no buzzing at all. No hum of protests like there was yesterday.

"Did anyone see what happened?" Nerdi asked.

"Cleo could tell you about the clues she saw if she calms down."

Nerdi spoke kindly to her new friend in the way Mama would speak to her bunnies when they were upset. "Cleo? I can't understand you if you don't calm down. Maybe I can help you figure out what happened to the queens and your friends, but you have to stop crying."

Cleo took a few deep breaths to pull herself together before saying, "Footprints. *Buzzzzzzzz. Sniffle.* Honey, *buzzzzzz*, in footprints. *Sniffle, buzzzzz.*"

Nerdi's whiskers twitched a few times and then stuck out stiff and straight. They were so stiff that Jimmy and Cleo could sit on them.

"Uh-oh," Nerdi said.

"The bunny twitch is back," said Jimmy. "What's the itch, bunny? Ya said uh-oh. What-oh?"

"Honey prints, you said? They were leading away from the hives?"

"Yeah," said Jimmy. "How did ya guess that?"

"There's only one group in Cottontail Burrow that leaves honey prints when they walk."

"Who's that?"

Nerdi gulped. "Bully bears!"

In This Together!

"What the heck is a bully bear?" Jimmy asked.

"Trouble," Nerdi sighed. "Bully bears live in a lair just outside the burrow."

Jimmy began to giggle.

"What's so funny, Jimmy?" Nerdi asked.

"Where do they live?"

"In a lair," Nerdi replied.

"A *bully bear lair?*" Jimmy flew around upside down in circles he was laughing so hard.

"I think he's in hysterics," Cleo said.

"Jimmy!" Nerdi yelled. "Pull yourself together! Bully bears are nothing to laugh at. They aren't very nice. They take things without asking, they are selfish, and no one has been able to have a civilized chat with them in years!"

"Yeah," Jimmy huffed. "They don't sound so tough!"

"Well, we need to find out where the bees are being kept in the lair. I'll go by myself. I don't want you guys to get taken, too, or hurt. Once I know where the queens are, we'll figure something out together."

"Nope. Your mama wouldn't like it if you got hurt. We can't let you go, at least not alone," Cleo said.

"We're friends," Jimmy added, "and Cleo and I are willing to do whatever it takes to help ya get the queens and the other bees back."

"Even if that means getting swatted," Cleo said as she puffed her fuzzy yellow chest out with pride. "If the bunny is going to be brave, we have to be brave too."

Nerdi, Jimmy, and Cleo traveled as a team to Bully Bear Lair. On their way they walked down the main street of town. During the later morning hours the shops would usually be filled with folks buying delicious fruits and veggies to prepare evening meals. The vendor carts that lined the street and were always stocked and overflowing with fruits and veggies were almost empty. An apple or two in this cart, a couple of carrots in that one, but Nerdi froze in her tracks as she saw the last cart, the one that held tomatoes. It was completely empty. She rocked back and forth on the heels of her paws and then everything went dark like before in her garden at home.

Jimmy and Cleo hovered over Nerdi, flapping their little bee wings as hard as they could to give her some air to wake her. The shock of the empty tomato bin caused Nerdi to faint in the middle of the street.

"Nerdi!" Cleo called. "Nerdi, wake up! Wake up, Nerdi, we need you! We can't do this alone."

"Bunny! Ya have to wake up or Cleo is gonna start crying again."

Nerdi could hear Jimmy and Cleo squabble about who was about to cry first. She didn't want her friends to fight about that and so she slowly fluttered open her eyes.

"C'mon, guys," Nerdi softly spoke. "We have to focus. Please don't fight."

"Nerdine!" Cleo buzzed with joy. "What happened?"

"All of a sudden you fainted and then we panicked. Sorry, bunny," said Jimmy.

"I'm sorry, too. This isn't about my favorite tomatoes," Nerdi said while her stomach grumbled. "It's about helping you guys." Nerdi picked herself up off the ground and dusted off her dress. "Let's go get the queens."

Into the Lair

DEEP IN THE WOODS OUTSIDE of Cottontail Burrow were a bunch of caves. These caves were known to everyone as the Bully Bear Lair. Mama told Nerdi that when she was a little bunny, these caves were full of angry bully bears. One day a bully bear cub was caught in a flood and the residents of Cottontail Burrow worked together to successfully rescue the cub. After that, many of the bully bears that lived in the caves decided that the residents of Cottontail Burrow weren't so bad after all. These bears left to come live peacefully in the burrow, all but three. The remaining bully bears blamed Cottontail Burrow for causing the flood and promised to make them miserable at every opportunity.

Jimmy, Cleo, and Nerdi hid in the cover of bushes around the last occupied cave of the Bully Bear Lair.

"Jimmy, you and Cleo stay here where it's safe," said Nerdi. "I'll go closer and see if I can see the queens and the other bees."

Nerdi carefully crept closer to the cave. She was able to get right up to the opening outside the cave. Inside, she could see three very large golden bears. They were sitting at a table that was covered with piles of honey jars!

"If they want to have a honey festival this year, they're all going to have to pay!" said the biggest bear. They all made a growly giggle that made the fur on the back of Nerdi's neck stand up.

"Work faster!" growled the biggest bear at the bees.

"We need to get these jars filled and taken back to the burrow by the end of the week! Make the honey faster!" grumbled the next biggest bear.

Nerdi could see the bees and the queens. They were kept in a hive that had six sides. The walls of the hive were thick glass that prevented the bees from getting out, but allowed the bears to watch them working. As the bees made honey the bears poked holes in the combs to release it. The pokes were very sharp and Nerdi could see a few bees with injured wings from the jabs. The honey dripped into a bucket and then the bears filled the jars on the table with that honey.

Nerdi was angry as she wondered how she was going to save the bees. "Terrible," Nerdi sighed to herself, or so she thought, and she put her paws over her mouth hoping the bears didn't hear her.

"What was that?" said the biggest bear.

"What was what?" replied the smallest.

"I heard someone say something," said the biggest bear.

"Of course you heard something, I'm talking to you!" yelled the second biggest bear. Bully bears also liked to bully each other. Nerdi used this moment to head back over to the bushes and tell Cleo and Jimmy what she saw.

Paying It Forward

As Cleo, Jimmy, and Nerdi walked back to town they threw out ideas on how to rescue the bees.

"Could we run in there and grab the hive?" Cleo asked.

"It looks very heavy," Nerdi responded, "and I don't think I would be able to carry it."

"Then I say we go in there, smash it open, and then the bees can fly and sting their way out," Jimmy suggested.

"I don't want to break the hive open. And besides, some of the bees are already hurt. I don't want any more to get hurt," Nerdi said.

By the time they reached her cottage, Nerdi didn't want to go inside. She had to figure this out. The bees were depending on her.

"Do you mind if we rest for a few minutes?" Nerdi asked.

"Sure, Nerdine. It's not even three and it feels like we've been at this forever. You rest. Jimmy and I will…" Cleo yawned. "We'll be right here."

"Yeah, we could use the rest, too." Nerdi stretched out underneath the willow tree. Jimmy and Cleo curled up to the pink bow on her ear. It wasn't long before Nerdi heard the bees catching some Z's. Nerdi loved the peace and quiet of the garden. It was her second favorite place to read and think. Nana Bunny currently napped in Nerdi's most favorite place—her chair. Yet under this beautiful willow tree Nerdi knew she could think of something great. Even though she didn't have tomatoes or honey, she felt very fortunate to have this beautiful garden all year long to think in.

"How am I going to help the bees?" Nerdi said to herself. "If I don't help the bees, the whole town will suffer and there will be no Honey Harvest Festival. I don't think that's ever happened before. Everyone will be so disappointed. I mean, that's just one of the things that make Cottontail Burrow so wonderful. We can harvest all year long because of the perfect weather. It's never too hot, it never gets cold, and…" In the middle of her thoughts, Nerdy gasped and her whiskers twitched. She reached up and removed her pink bow with her two bee buddies resting in the folds and carefully held them in her paws.

"Cleo. Jimmy—wake up! I know how we can save the queens!"

Cleo and Jimmy yawned and stretched. "What was that, Nerdine?" Cleo asked.

"I think she said she knows how to get the queens and our buzzies back. What's the plan, bunny?" said Jimmy.

"I'll tell you all about it on the way back to town. We have to go see a penguin about a snow cone!" Nerdi sprinted to town with jackrabbit speed. Cleo and Jimmy didn't want to fly to keep up, so they hung onto the pink bow on her ear.

"I don't get it. How's a snow cone going to help us get the queens back?" asked Jimmy.

"Not just one snow cone," Nerdi answered. "But a snow cone machine!"

"Okay, now I don't get it," said Cleo.

"Why do the bees live here?" asked Nerdi.

"The weather here creates perfect working conditions. We can be busy bees all year."

"Exactly! Bees can work all year long in Cottontail Burrow because there's no winter! Everything is in season here because we skip a lot of seasons! And because there's no winter the bears don't hibernate!"

"Bunny, that is genius!" Jimmy buzzed.

"To get the bully bears to hibernate we need the snow cone machine to make it snow AROUND their lair!"

"I have to admit, that's a clever idea," said Cleo. "Do you think the penguins will help us?"

"I know they will! They care about what's been happening around here, and they need honey, too."

When they reached the penguin snow parlor, Nerdi explained her idea to the penguins who were very excited to help and donate carts to the cause. They wanted to return the favor to thank Nerdi for her help when they were sick with the flu, so helping Nerdi and the bees was just paying it forward.

"For this to work," Nerdi said, "the snow cone machine is going to need a few temporary adjustments." The penguins helped Nerdi attach a tube that connected to three large fans outside the carts. Instead of keeping the snow inside the cart's freezer to be scooped out for snow cones, it would be blown out to create the illusion that it was snowing outside the Bully Bear Lair.

"Do you think this will work?" asked Jimmy.

"No," said Nerdi, "nothing is ever one hundred percent, but I'm very confident."

Busting Loose!

EARLY THE NEXT MORNING, NERDI, the penguins with the snow carts, and Jimmy and Cleo returned to the Bully Bear Lair. The penguins started to surround the lair with the snow cone carts. Nerdi worried that they were making too much noise.

"Five dollars," the biggest bear growled from the cave. "We won't make enough money if we only sell it for five dollars! We got the only bees in the whole burrow who are making honey right now. Folks will pay whatever we say—top dollar! So we should be asking for six dollars!"

"Bully bears must be terrible at math," whispered Cleo.

"What they lack in intelligence they make up for in meanness," Nerdi replied.

Fortunately for them, this heated debate on pricing distracted the bears from what was happening outside their lair. The penguins finally positioned the snow carts and waited for Nerdi to give the signal.

"Once they see it's snowing we just have to wait for them to fall asleep. Then we'll slip inside, get the bees, and get out fast before they wake up." Nerdi gave the first signal and the penguins revved up their machines. They put the setting on blizzard and then ducked out of sight.

The smallest bear noticed the change in weather first. "Hey, guys? Did the weather say anything about snow?"

"Don't be ridiculous," growled the biggest bear. "It doesn't snow here! Maybe the trees have dandruff."

"Now who sounds ridiculous," replied the smallest bear. "Trees don't get dandruff! Look!"

The smallest bear pointed to the window. The biggest bear looked away in disgust from what he was doing and then stuck his head out the cave. "Maybe it will pass quickly. I wouldn't worry about it."

"Yes," said the second biggest bear, "but it's really coming down out there. We might have to settle in for winter."

"Winter? We haven't settled in for a winter's nap in years!" grumbled the biggest bear as the smallest bear yawned. "Don't start yawning! If you yawn," he yawned, "then the rest of us will start," he yawned again, "yawning!" It didn't take long for the lair to be surrounded by snow. The more it snowed, the louder the yawning that came from the cave. After a few minutes, the yawns turned to snores.

"Whoa," said Jimmy, "it worked! The bunny's plan worked!"

"It's not over yet, Jimmy," said Cleo. "We still have to get the bees out."

Nerdi signaled the penguins to shut off the snow machines. Cleo and Jimmy flew around to the opening to make sure the bears were asleep. The two smaller bears were curled up in bed holding stuffed Goldilocks dolls. The biggest bear was stretched out on the floor like a rug. In the back of the lair they could see the glass hive on a table where the bees were being held prisoner. When they saw Jimmy and Cleo flying toward them, they began to buzz with excitement.

"Shhhhhhh," buzzed Cleo. "We're going to get you all out, but you have to be very quiet."

Jimmy flew back to the opening and signaled to Nerdi that the bears were out cold. It was a warm day and the fresh fallen snow already began to melt. Nerdi had to work fast because the bears could wake up at any moment. She hopped quickly through the snow. She had eaten snow before as one of the treats from the ice cream shop, but she didn't like it on her feet. She entered the lair. The biggest bear was huge—so big that he took up most of the floor. Nerdi barely had anywhere to step. When she reached the table, she tried to lift the hive.

"It's too heavy for me to carry. You guys are going to have to fly out."

"They can't fly," whispered Jimmy. "The bears have been keeping their wings wet so they can't fly out when they take the honey. You're gonna have to carry them out."

Nerdi knew she had only one chance to get the bees out safely, but she didn't know these bees. Would they sting her? She didn't see any of the fancy caps like the one Cleo would wear. The queen honeybee motioned for her to come closer.

"I can see that you are frightened. But you have my word these bees will not hurt you. Queen's honor."

Nerdi had to let go of her fear once again. She carefully took the lid off the glass hive. Cleo and Jimmy helped the queens and the other bees climb out and Nerdi put them wherever she had space. There were bees in her pockets, bees on her ears, bees on the bows, bees in her paws, and bees near her toes. Not a single bee was to be left behind. Once everyone was out, Jimmy and Cleo led the way to safety. Nerdi stepped as carefully as she could. She made it past the smallest bears still sound asleep in their bed. She almost made it past the biggest bear that was laid out like a rug.

"GRRRRRRRRRRRRRRRRRRRRR!" he growled when Nerdi stepped on his paw. "WHERE DO YOU THINK YOU'RE GOING WITH OUR BEES?!" The bear rug stood up.

"Run for it, Nerdi!" Jimmy yelled. He and Cleo were waiting just outside the entrance to the lair. The bees Nerdi carried held on as she bounded as fast as she could toward the exit. Half asleep, the biggest bear chased her. As Nerdi ran, the penguins assembled at the front of the cave with the snow machines.

"Change the settings to snowball," Cleo yelled.

As Nerdi made it out, Jimmy yelled, "NOW!" The penguins turned on all the machines at once and they shot snowballs at the biggest bear. Some of the snowballs hit him and the ones that didn't began to quickly pile high in front of the lair, trapping the bears inside. Once the entire cave was covered the penguins turned off the machines and the bees cheered. They were finally going home. Inside, under all the tightly packed snow, you could hear the bears growling and snarling in between saying some very awful things about bunnies, and then silence, followed by the sounds of snoring.

Tomatoes and Honey—Thanks, Nerdi Bunny!

THE NEXT DAY NERDI AND the queens met with the mayor and President O'Llama, who was in Cottontail Burrow for his vacation and to help plan activities for the festival. After hours of discussion they wrote a list of rules that would be known as the Bee Bill. Everyone in Cottontail Burrow came to the square to hear the news. Jimmy, Cleo, and the two queens sat on Nerdi's shoulder as she stood next to the mayor while President O'Llama made the announcement.

"Residents of Cottontail Burrow, I am pleased to announce that as of noon today, the bees will return to work. If we want the bees to do their job then the community must do theirs, and that is to treat them with the dignity and respect that they deserve. This morning, with the help of Nerdine Bunny, we created the Bee Bill. I am sure that if we follow this guide, we can all live and work together in harmony."

Everyone in the square applauded and cheered. Mama, who returned yesterday, smiled with pride while Artsy and Sporty clapped and cheered the loudest.

"Is there anything that you would like to say, Nerdine?" asked the president.

Nerdi nervously approached the podium. What could she add? How could she follow the president? A slow hush came over the crowd. Nerdi thought for a moment and then added, "It's important to remember that many bees are really nice, so let them work and do not swat. Please follow that advice. Thank you."

That afternoon the bees went back to work around the clock for the next few weeks to make up for lost time. Residents of Cottontail Burrow made sure the bees had plenty of sugar water to drink and safe places to rest. On the morning of the Honey and Harvest Festival, Nerdi hoppily got up and went out into the garden to get tomatoes for her ice cream entry. When she reached the tomato plants, it was a very different situation than it was just a few weeks ago. Nerdi was in tomato heaven! Every plant in her yard was covered in ripe, delicious tomatoes and Nerdi felt like she was floating. Just as she was about to start picking…

"Stop! Wait!" came two voices from the garden. It was Cleo and Jimmy.

"What's wrong? Is everything okay? Did the bears wake up?"

"Nah, the bears are still napping in their igloo. The president and the penguins are making sure of that," said Jimmy.

"Nothing is wrong, Nerdi," said Cleo. "We just wanted to come by and say thank you for your help."

The garden buzzed and she was surrounded by hundreds of bees. Not like before with anger, but with a dance and chants to what Jimmy called the "Bumble Honey Boogie":

When Cottontail Burrow
Was down to zero,
The queens were taken.
The bees needed a hero,
The shops all closed,
And that wasn't funny.
But she got us back to work
And now everything's sunny!
Tomatoes and honey, thanks to Nerdi Bunny!
Tomatoes and honey, thanks to Nerdi Bunny!"

The queens from the hives appeared and sat in Nerdi's paw.

"Nerdine, on behalf of the bees of Cottontail Burrow, we want to thank you for what you've done. Please accept this small token of our gratitude."

The bees hushed their chanting to a whisper and opened the circle that surrounded Nerdi. Jimmy and Cleo flew forward and several bees carried the largest, reddest, juiciest tomato Nerdi had ever seen!

"Don't pass out again, bunny!" buzzed Jimmy. "Everyone pitched in to work on it for ya for the festival."

"Do you think you can make something delicious with that?" asked Cleo.

"Thank you very much, bees. And yes, I think I can make something VERY delicious with this," Nerdi replied.

"Very good then," said the queens. "Back to work, bees!" they commanded and the bees dispersed into their regular routine.

"See ya around, bunny," said Jimmy as he gave Nerdi a hug on her nose.

"Try to win today," said Cleo as she waved good-bye, and then she and Jimmy buzzed out of sight.

Mama, Sporty, and Artsy couldn't believe their eyes when Nerdi came in carrying such a gorgeous tomato.

"I think that may be the biggest tomato I have ever seen," said Mama.

Nerdi got to work right away mixing ingredients for her tomato ice cream entry for the festival. She didn't use the whole tomato since there was so much of it. She decided to share it with her family for the salad they would eat at the festival picnic.

At the Honey and Harvest Festival every treat you could possibly want to eat in Cottontail Burrow was there thanks to the bees: tomato chips, honey cakes, apple ale, berry pies, and pecan tarts. The judges awarded Nerdi first prize for her tomato ice cream, saying it was "refreshing and full of flavor." Mama, Artsy, Sporty, and Nerdi enjoyed the winning ice cream at the picnic along with their favorite tomato and basil salad.

And they all agreed it was the best lunch they ever ate.

Three Easy Ways That YOU

Can Help the Bees!

1. Plant bee gardens with things like mint, summer squash, strawberries, lavender, marigolds, chives, clover, thyme, sage, rosemary, and catmint.
2. Don't pick the dandelions! People may not like these weeds, but if bees come out early, these tough flowers provide them with food before the other plants and flowers bloom later in the spring and summer.
3. NO PESTICIDES ON YOUR GARDENS! When we use this on our plants, and the bees come in contact with it, the bees become very sick and they die.

Thank you for reading Nerdi's first adventure!

If you liked the story, please leave us a review on Amazon and Goodreads.

Check out our other titles and join Nerdi as she travels to Chew Orleans in...

Nerdi Bunny
and the
Big Bayou Gator Grief

Written by Aisha Toombs
Illustrated by Michael Morris

You can also connect with Nerdi Bunny and author Aisha Toombs on social media:

Twitter: @NerdiBunny & @AishaToombs77

Instagram: @nerdi.bunny & @anicole1977

Or visit our website www.NerdiBunny.com

CPSIA information can be obtained
at www.ICGtesting.com
Printed in the USA
BVHW041737030220
571298BV00008B/391

9 781733 794701